FOODS OF MEXICO

by Christine Velure Roholt

BELLWETHER MEDIA • MINNEAPOLIS, MN

Library of Congress Cataloging-in-Publication Data

VeLure Roholt, Christine, author.
　Foods of Mexico / by Christine VeLure Roholt.
　　　pages cm. -- (Express. Cook with Me)
　Summary: "Information accompanies step-by-step instructions on how to cook Mexican food. The text level and subject matter are intended for students in grades 3 through 7"-- Provided by publisher.
　Audience: Age 7-12.
　Audience: Grades 3-7.
　Includes bibliographical references and index.
　ISBN 978-1-62617-121-3 (hardcover : alk. paper)
 1. Cooking, Mexican--Juvenile literature. 2. Food habits--Mexico--Juvenile literature. 3. Mexico--Social life and customs--Juvenile literature. I. Title.
　TX716.M4V47 2014
　641.5972--dc23
　　　　　　　　　　　　　　2014008282

This edition first published in 2015 by Bellwether Media, Inc.

No part of this publication may be reproduced in whole or in part without written permission of the publisher. For information regarding permission, write to Bellwether Media, Inc., Attention: Permissions Department, 5357 Penn Avenue South, Minneapolis, MN 55419.

Text copyright © 2015 by Bellwether Media, Inc. PILOT, EXPRESS, and associated logos are trademarks and/or registered trademarks of Bellwether Media, Inc. SCHOLASTIC, CHILDREN'S PRESS, and associated logos are trademarks and/or registered trademarks of Scholastic Inc.

Printed in the United States of America, North Mankato, MN.

Table of Contents

Cooking the Mexican Way   4
Eating the Mexican Way   6
Regional Foods   8
Sips and Sweets   10
Getting Ready to Cook   12
Tortillas   14
Enfrijoladas   16
Esquites   18
Sopa de Tortilla   20
Glossary   22
To Learn More   23
Index   24

Cooking the Mexican Way

Modern Mexican **cuisine** still reflects the cooking practices of the past. Recipes and preparation techniques have been handed down by families for **generations**. Many of these were used by **native** peoples hundreds of years ago. Others came from early Spanish **settlers**. The strong sense of **tradition** and community in Mexican culture keeps these methods alive.

Corn, beans, and chiles form the center of Mexican cooking. Native communities farmed these before the Spanish settled in the area. Fresh, local ingredients, such as tomatoes and avocados, add variety to the basics. Mexican people often use many different parts of a crop, including cornhusks and banana leaves. The cooks in a family or community prepare the meal together. Food is most often steamed, fried, grilled, or boiled.

Old School
Some cooks still prefer to cook over an open fire. They believe this gives the best flavor.

Eating the Mexican Way

Eating is a social activity in Mexico. People gather with friends and family to share a meal and linger long after the food is finished. The main meal is in the middle of the day. Families often come home from work or school to spend it together.

Hands Up!

It is impolite to keep hands under the table during a meal. Mexican people rest their wrists on the edge of the table. Putting elbows on the table is also considered impolite.

Before the meal, Mexican people say *"buen provecho"* to the other diners. This means "enjoy your meal." Then they wait to take their first bites until the host begins to eat. When they are finished, Mexican people leave a little food on their plates. This shows they are satisfied. After eating, they relax and chat with each other in a tradition called *sobremesa*.

Regional Foods

Mexico is made up of 31 states and many smaller regions. Strong traditions distinguish these communities from each other in both culture and cooking. Even if two areas share a recipe, they might have different ideas about how to prepare the food.

Where is Mexico?

Nuevo León
machaca con huevo: Dried, shredded beef mixed with egg, tomato, and onion

Veracruz
huachinang a la Veracruzana: Red snapper baked in a sauce of tomatoes, onions, and herbs

Yucatán
cochinita pibil: Pulled pork slow-roasted in a banana leaf

Puebla
chiles en nogada: Poblano chili peppers stuffed with meat, fruit, and nuts, covered in a walnut cream sauce and topped with pomegranate

Oaxaca
mole negro: Chili-chocolate sauce often served over meat or tamales

Sips and Sweets

In Mexico, drinks often rely on the wealth of local ingredients. Sweet *agua frescas* usually accompany a meal. They are water **infused** with fresh fruit, seeds, or flowers. One of the most common is *horchata*, a creamy agua fresca made with rice and cinnamon. Mexican people also sip on foamy hot chocolate with a hint of chile. This sweet treat has its roots in the Aztec culture of the 1400s and 1500s.

agua frescas

flan

High Cost

The Aztecs considered cacao beans to be so valuable that they used them as currency.

For dessert, Mexican people can choose from a variety of sweets. *Tres leches* is a popular summer treat. This sponge cake is soaked in three different types of milk and served chilled. *Flan* is another traditional Mexican dessert. It is baked **custard** covered in a caramel sauce. Those looking for something lighter find a *paleta* from a street cart. This ice pop is made from fresh fruit.

Getting Ready to Cook

Before you begin cooking, read these safety reminders. Make sure you also read the recipes you will follow. You will want to gather all the ingredients and cooking tools right away.

Safety Reminders

 Ask an adult for permission to start cooking. An adult should be near when you use kitchen appliances or a sharp knife.

 Wash your hands with soapy water before you start cooking. Wash your hands again if you lick your fingers or handle raw meat.

 If you have long hair, tie it back. Remove any bracelets or rings that you have on.

 Wear an apron when you cook. It will protect food from dirt and your clothes from spills and splatters.

 Always use oven mitts when handling hot cookware. If you accidentally burn yourself, run the burned area under cold water and tell an adult.

 If a fire starts, call an adult immediately. Never throw water on a fire. Baking soda can smother small flames. A lid can put out a fire in a pot or pan. If flames are large and leaping, call 911 and leave the house.

 Clean up the kitchen when you are done cooking. Make sure all appliances are turned off.

Tortillas
tor–TEE–yahs

Did You Know? The word tortilla comes from the Spanish word meaning "round cake."

Thin Mexican Flatbread
Makes 12

Tortillas have been a **staple** of Mexican cooking for thousands of years. They are traditionally made with flour in northern Mexico. In many areas of Mexico and South America, they are also made with corn.

What You'll Need

- 2 cups flour
- 1/2 teaspoon salt
- 1 teaspoon baking powder
- 1 tablespoon lard (substitute: margarine)
- 3/4 cup water
- shredded cheese (optional)
- whisk
- large bowl
- rolling pin
- large frying pan

Let's Make It!

1
Combine the flour, salt, and baking powder in a large bowl, then use your fingers to mix in the lard.

2
Add the water to the mixture, then knead with your hands until it becomes dough.

3
On a lightly floured surface, knead the dough until it becomes smooth and elastic.

4
Divide the dough into 12 equal pieces, then roll them into balls.

5
Use a floured rolling pin to roll the dough into small, thin slices.

6
Place a frying pan on medium-high heat, then set a tortilla on the hot surface. Cook until it bubbles and is golden on one side, then flip the tortilla and cook it until the other side is golden. Repeat.

Enjoy!

Cover the cooked tortillas with a paper towel to keep them warm, then serve with cheese, vegetables, meat, or beans to create tacos or quesadillas!

Make Quesadillas

Combine your tortillas with shredded cheese to make your own quesadilla:

1. Place one cooked tortilla in a frying pan over medium heat.
2. Cover the tortilla with the shredded cheese. Then place another cooked tortilla on top.
3. Cook for about 1 minute, then flip to cook the other side until the cheese is melted.

Enfrijoladas
en-free-hole-LA-duhs

Did You Know?
Enfrijoladas get their name from the Spanish word *frijol*, which means "beans."

Bean-covered Tortillas
Serves 4

Enfrijoladas are a popular dish all around Mexico. They are served for breakfast, lunch, or as a light dinner. People eat them plain or topped with eggs, meat, and vegetables.

What You'll Need

- 1 small onion
- 1 garlic clove
- 1 tablespoon olive oil
- 2 cups black beans (substitute: pinto beans)
- 1/2 cup sour cream
- 1/2 cup crumbled queso fresco
- chopped cilantro
- 8 tortillas
- knife
- saucepan
- blender or food processor
- large frying pan
- plate
- spatula

Let's Make It!

1
Finely chop the onion and the garlic.

2
Pour the olive oil in a saucepan and place on medium heat. Sauté the onion for 5 minutes or until soft, then add the garlic and cook another 30 seconds.

3
Put the onion, garlic, and beans in a blender or food processor, then puree until smooth.

4
Pour the mixture into a saucepan on medium heat to warm the beans.

5
Place a tortilla in a large frying pan on low heat, then warm for about 30 seconds on each side.

6
Transfer the tortilla to a plate, then spread a thin layer of the bean puree on the tortilla.

7
Fold the tortilla in half.

8
Add the sour cream, cheese, and chopped cilantro.

Enjoy!

Esquites
es-KEY-tays

Mexican Corn Salad
Serves 4

Esquites are a popular, easy-to-make snack. They are commonly sold in markets, restaurants, and from streetside carts throughout Mexico.

What You'll Need

- 2 tablespoons butter (substitute: olive oil)
- 3 cups corn
- 1 green bell pepper
- 1-2 chopped garlic cloves
- 2 tablespoons mayonnaise
- 2 ounces crumbled queso fresco
- 1-2 chopped green onions (optional)
- 2 tablespoons chopped cilantro (optional)
- chili powder
- knife
- large frying pan
- large bowl
- spoon

18

Let's Make It!

1
Place a large frying pan over medium-high heat, then add the butter.

2
Add the corn, then cook for 5–10 minutes or until blackened.

3
Finely chop the green pepper and remove its seeds, then add it to the corn. Cook for 1 minute.

4
Transfer the corn to a large bowl.

5
Mix in the garlic, mayonnaise, cheese, onions, and cilantro.

6
Add the chili powder to taste, then serve warm.

Most Popular Crop

Corn is the most popular crop grown in Mexico. Farmers plant more than 40 different types of corn.

Sopa de Tortilla
SO-pa de tor-TEE-ya

Mexican Tortilla Soup
Serves 4

Sopa de tortilla was likely first made in central Mexico. Today, it is a favorite dish all around the country.

What You'll Need

- 1 tablespoon olive oil
- 1 chopped onion
- 2 chopped garlic cloves
- 1 cup chopped vegetables (recommended: corn, zucchini, and red peppers)
- 3 medium tomatoes
- 4 ounces green chiles
- 1 1/2 cups cooked shredded chicken (optional)
- 6 cups chicken stock (substitute: vegetable stock)
- 2-3 corn tortillas
- 1 avocado
- lime wedges
- sour cream
- 1 cup queso fresco
- knife
- large saucepan
- baking sheet
- spatula
- ladle

Let's Make It!

1

Pour the olive oil in a saucepan on medium-high heat, then sauté the onion, garlic, and vegetables.

2

Add the tomatoes, chiles, and chicken, then pour in the chicken stock. Bring the soup to a boil, then simmer for 20 minutes.

3

Preheat the oven to 400 degrees Fahrenheit, then use a knife to cut the tortillas into strips.

4

Place the tortilla strips on a baking sheet, then bake for about 5 minutes. Remove the baking sheet from the oven, then use a spatula to flip the tortilla strips. Bake the tortillas until golden brown on the edges.

5

Transfer the tortilla strips to a plate, then use a knife to chop the avocado and lime.

6

Ladle the soup into bowls and top with the tortilla strips, then add the sour cream, cheese, avocado, and lime wedges.

Did You Know?

Another name for tortilla soup is *Sopa Azteca*, or "Aztec soup."

21

Glossary

cuisine—a style of cooking unique to a certain area or group of people

custard—a pudding-like dessert made with eggs and milk

generations—groups of family members that have a wide range of ages

infused—has absorbed the flavors of something

native—originally from a specific place

settlers—people who go to live in a new place where few or no other people live

staple—a food that is widely and regularly eaten

tradition—a custom, idea, or belief that has been passed down from one generation to the next

To Learn More

AT THE LIBRARY

McCulloch, Julie. *Mexico*. Chicago, Ill.: Heinemann Library, 2009.

Sexton, Colleen. *Mexico*. Minneapolis, Minn.: Bellwether Media, 2011.

Wagner, Lisa. *Cool Mexican Cooking: Fun and Tasty Recipes for Kids*. Minneapolis, Minn.: ABDO Pub., 2011.

ON THE WEB

Learning more about Mexico is as easy as 1, 2, 3.

1. Go to www.factsurfer.com.

2. Enter "Mexico" into the search box.

3. Click the "Surf" button and you will see a list of related web sites.

With factsurfer.com, finding more information is just a click away.

Index

Aztecs, 10, 11, 21
beverages, 10
corn, 5, 19
customs, 5, 6, 7
desserts, 11
enfrijoladas, 16-17
esquites, 18-19
influences, 4
ingredients, 5, 10, 19
location, 8
manners, 6, 7
preparation, 12
regional foods, 8-9
safety, 13
sopa de tortilla, 20-21
techniques, 4, 5
tortillas, 14-15

The images in this book are reproduced through the courtesy of: Shutterstock, front cover; Maria Komar, title page; bonchan, credits page, p. 20; optimarc, table of contents; Solphoto, pp. 4-5; Danny Lehman/ Glow Images, p. 5; Armadillo Stock, p. 6; Kablonk/ Glow Images, p. 7; Peter Kim, p. 9 (top, middle right); Corbis/ SuperStock, p. 9 (middle left); Nathalie Speliers Ufermann, p. 9 (bottom left); Judith Haden/ Danita Delimont/ Newscom, p. 9 (bottom right); Africa Studio, pp. 10, 13; Lesya Dolyuk, p. 11 (left); stockcreations, p. 11 (right); Arina P Habich, p. 12 (left); Jose Luis Pelaez, Inc/ Corbis/ Glow Images, p. 12 (right); travellight, p. 14; Jiri Hera, p. 14 (small); picturepartners, p. 16 (small); daffodilred, p. 17 (small); v.s.anandhakrishna, p. 18 (small); Yasonya, p. 19 (bottom); Charlie Neuman/ Newscom, p. 21 (bottom); VladislavGudovskiy, p. 21 (bottom right); baibaz, p. 22; all other photos courtesy of bswing.